WINNIE-THE-POOH'S
Book of Spring

A. A. MILNE

WINNIE-THE-POOH'S
Book of Spring

with decorations by ERNEST H. SHEPARD

Dutton Children's Books • NEW YORK

Published in the United States by Dutton Children's Books,
a division of Penguin Putnam Books for Young Readers
345 Hudson Street, New York, New York 10014

Designed by Daniel Hosek

Manufactured in China
First Edition
ISBN 0-525-46819-6

A Springtime Stroll

It was a fine spring morning in the forest as Pooh started out. Little soft clouds played happily in a blue sky, skipping from time to time in front of the sun as if they had come to put it out, and then sliding away suddenly so that the next might have his turn. Through them and between them the sun shone bravely; and a copse which had worn its firs all the year round seemed old and dowdy now beside the new green lace which the beeches had put on so prettily.

Winnie-the-Pooh

Daffodowndilly

She wore her yellow sun-bonnet,
  She wore her greenest gown;
She turned to the south wind
  And curtsied up and down.
She turned to the sunlight
  And shook her yellow head,
And whispered to her neighbour:
  "Winter is dead."

When We Were Very Young

Noise, By Pooh

Oh, the butterflies are flying,
Now the winter days are dying,
And the primroses are trying
     To be seen.

And the cows are almost cooing,
And the turtle-doves are mooing,
Which is why a Pooh is poohing
     In the sun.

For the spring is really springing;
You can see a skylark singing,
And the blue-bells, which are ringing,
     Can be heard.

And the cuckoo isn't cooing,
But he's cucking and he's ooing,
And a Pooh is simply poohing
     Like a bird.

The House At Pooh Corner

Spring Morning

Where am I going? I don't quite know.
Down to the stream where the king-cups
    grow—
Up on the hill where the pine-trees blow—
Anywhere, anywhere. *I* don't know.

Where am I going? The clouds sail by,
Little ones, baby ones, over the sky.
Where am I going? The shadows pass,
Little ones, baby ones, over the grass.

When We Were Very Young

Twinkletoes

When the sun
Shines through the leaves of the apple-tree,
When the sun
Makes shadows of the leaves of the apple-tree,
Then I pass
On the grass
From one leaf to another,
From one leaf to its brother,
Tip-toe, tip-toe!
Here I go!

When We Were Very Young

The Engineer

Let it rain!
Who cares?
I've a train
Upstairs,
With a brake
Which I make
From a string
Sort of thing,
Which works
In jerks,
'Cos it drops
In the spring.

Now We Are Six

Rain, Rain, Rain

Christopher Robin lived at the very top of the Forest. It rained, and it rained, and it rained, but the water couldn't come up to *his* house. Every morning he went out with his umbrella and put a stick in the place where the water came up to, and every next morning he went out and couldn't see his stick any more, so he put another stick in the place where the water came up to, and then he walked home again.

Winnie-the-Pooh

The Invaders

Along the narrow carpet ride,
With primroses on either side,
Between their shadows and the sun,
The cows came slowly, one by one,
Breathing the early morning air
And leaving it still sweeter there.

But all the little wood was still,
As if it waited so, until
Some blackbird on an outpost yew,
Watching the slow procession through,
Lifted his yellow beak at last
To whistle that the line had passed....
Then all the wood began to sing
Its morning anthem to the spring.

When We Were Very Young

Violets for Eeyore

Piglet had got up early that morning to pick himself a bunch of violets; and when he had picked them and put them in a pot in the middle of his house, it suddenly came over him that nobody had ever picked Eeyore a bunch of violets, and the more he thought of this, the more he thought how sad it was to be an Animal who had never had a bunch of violets picked for him.

The House At Pooh Corner

Beside the Bridge

Christopher Robin came down from the Forest to the
bridge, feeling all sunny and careless, and just as if twice
nineteen didn't matter a bit, as it didn't on such a happy
afternoon, and he thought that if he stood on the bottom
rail of the bridge, and leant over, and watched the river
slipping slowly away beneath him, then he would suddenly
know everything that there was to be known, and he would
be able to tell Pooh, who wasn't quite sure about some of it.

The House At Pooh Corner

Water-Lilies

Where the water-lilies go
To and fro,
Rocking in the ripples of the water,
Lazy on a leaf lies the Lake King's daughter,
And the faint winds shake her.
Who will come and take her?
I will! I will!

When We Were Very Young

Wondering

The Piglet was sitting on the ground at the door of his house blowing happily at a dandelion, and wondering whether it would be this year, next year, sometime or never. He had just discovered that it would be never, and was trying to remember what *"it"* was, and hoping it wasn't anything nice.

Winnie-the-Pooh

Swing Song

Here I go up in my swing
    Ever so high.
I am the King of the fields, and the King
    Of the town.
I am the King of the earth, and the King
    Of the sky.
Here I go up in my swing…
    Now I go down.

Now We Are Six

Paying a Call

Rabbit hurried on by the edge of the Hundred Acre Wood, feeling more important every minute, and soon he came to the tree where Christopher Robin lived. He knocked at the door, and he called out once or twice, and then he walked back a little way and put his paw up to keep the sun out, and called to the top of the tree, and then he turned all round and shouted "Hallo!" and "I say!" "It's Rabbit!"— but nothing happened. Then he stopped and listened, and everything stopped and listened with him, and the Forest was very lone and still and peaceful in the sunshine, until suddenly a hundred miles above him a lark began to sing.

The House At Pooh Corner

Buttercup Days

What has she got in that little brown head?
Wonderful thoughts which can never be said.
What has she got in that firm little fist of hers?
Somebody's thumb, and it feels like Christopher's.

    Where is Anne?
    Close to her man.
    Brown head, gold head,
      In and out the buttercups.

Now We Are Six

Digging a Small Hole

Piglet was busy digging a small hole in the ground outside his house.

"Hallo, Piglet," said Pooh.

"Hallo, Pooh," said Piglet, giving a jump of surprise. "I knew it was you."

"So did I," said Pooh. "What are you doing?"

"I'm planting a haycorn, Pooh, so that it can grow up into an oak-tree, and have lots of haycorns just outside the front door instead of having to walk miles and miles, do you see, Pooh?"

"Supposing it doesn't?" said Pooh.

"It will, because Christopher Robin says it will, so that's why I'm planting it."

The House At Pooh Corner

The Scent of May

One day when the sun had come back over the Forest, bringing with it the scent of May, and all the streams of the Forest were tinkling happily to find themselves their own pretty shape again, and the little pools lay dreaming of the life they had seen and the big things they had done, and in the warmth and quiet of the Forest the cuckoo was trying over his voice carefully and listening to see if he liked it, and wood-pigeons were complaining gently to themselves in their lazy comfortable way that it was the other fellow's fault, but it didn't matter very much; on such a day as this Christopher Robin whistled in a special way he had, and Owl came flying out of the Hundred Acre Wood to see what was wanted.

Winnie-the-Pooh

Happiness

John had
Great Big
Waterproof
Boots on;
John had a
Great Big
Waterproof
Hat;
John had a
Great Big
Waterproof
Mackintosh—
And that
(Said John)
Is
That.

When We Were Very Young

Up in a Tree

"Hallo, Roo!" called Piglet. "What are you doing?"

"We can't get down, we can't get down!" cried Roo. "Isn't it fun? Pooh, isn't it fun, Tigger and I are living in a tree, like Owl, and we're going to stay here for ever and ever. I can see Piglet's house. Piglet, I can see your house from here. Aren't we high? Is Owl's house as high up as this?"

"How did you get there, Roo?" asked Piglet.

"On Tigger's back!"

The House At Pooh Corner

A Delightfully Warm Day

The sun was so delightfully warm, and the stone, which had been sitting in it for a long time, was so warm, too, that Pooh had almost decided to go on being Pooh in the middle of the stream for the rest of the morning, when he remembered Rabbit.

"Rabbit," said Pooh to himself. "I *like* talking to Rabbit. He talks about sensible things. He doesn't use long, difficult words, like Owl. He uses short, easy words, like 'What about lunch?' and 'Help yourself, Pooh.' I suppose *really,* I ought to go and see Rabbit."

The House At Pooh Corner

The Old Grey Donkey

The old grey donkey, Eeyore, stood by himself in a thistly corner of the forest, his front feet well apart, his head on one side, and thought about things. Sometimes he thought sadly to himself, "Why?" and sometimes he thought, "Wherefore?" and sometimes he thought, "Inasmuch as which?"—and sometimes he didn't quite know what he *was* thinking about. So when Winnie-the-Pooh came stumping along, Eeyore was very glad to be able to stop thinking for a little, in order to say "How do you do?" in a gloomy manner to him.

Winnie-the-Pooh

Waiting at the Window

These are my two drops of rain
Waiting on the window-pane.

I am waiting here to see
Which the winning one will be.

Both of them have different names.
One is John and one is James.

All the best and all the worst
Comes from which of them is first.

James has met a sort of smear.
John is getting very near.

Is he going fast enough?
(James has found a piece of fluff.)

John has hurried quickly by.
(James was talking to a fly.)

John is there, and John has won!
Look! I told you! Here's the sun!

Now We Are Six